CONSCIOUS CULTURE
PUBLISHING

For

Teachers everywhere educating the youth

Conscious Culture Publishing
Text & illustrations copyright © 2019 by Marlon McKenney
All rights reserved. No part of the contents of this book may be reproduced by any means without the written permission of the publisher.
978-1-7322051-5-4

E-Book & Softcover also Available:

www.consciousculturepublishing.com
www.facebook.com/ConsciousCultr
@ConsciousCultr

The illustrations were created digitally using a variety of software platforms including Cinema 4D, Photoshop, and After Effects.

First Edition
10 9 8 7 6 5 4 3 2 1

Conscious Culture Publishing is an independent publishing company committed to creating a platform for diverse content that push the boundaries of traditional storytelling.
Through the creation of narratives that are a reflection of the people both creating and experiencing these stories, we empower young readers to reach their fullest potential while embracing their history and culture.

THE GENIUS OF EGYPT

Written & Illustrated by:

Marlon McKenney

Edited by:

Julia Akpan

Within the eternal darkness of the Universe,
there is a divine and mystical light that shines
through the shadows.

Since the beginning of time, this extraordinary light
has brought knowledge, wisdom, and understanding
to the entire world.

Over 4000 years ago in Africa,
this powerful light was used to
discover mathematics, architecture,
science, and magic.

In the mysterious kingdom of Egypt,
once known as Kemet,
a brilliant young African became
the light of a vast empire;
destined to be celebrated for eternity.

His name was Imhotep.

Imhotep grew up in ancient *Kemet,* around 2600 BC, in the capital city of *Memphis.* His father, *Kanofer,* was a skilled architect and master builder known for designing beautiful temples throughout the kingdom. Kanofer wanted nothing more than to pass his vast knowledge down to his son.

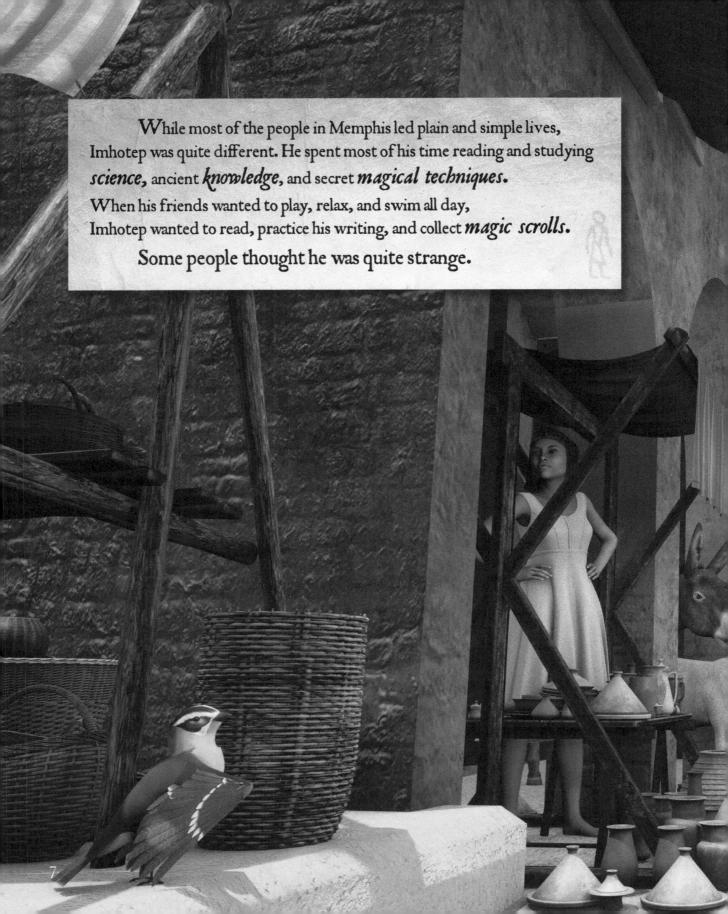

While most of the people in Memphis led plain and simple lives, Imhotep was quite different. He spent most of his time reading and studying *science*, ancient *knowledge*, and secret *magical techniques*.

When his friends wanted to play, relax, and swim all day, Imhotep wanted to read, practice his writing, and collect *magic scrolls*.

Some people thought he was quite strange.

Imhotep lived along a great river called the *Nile*. Every spring the river would rise and rise until it flooded the surrounding farmland.

Days later the water would recede and leave behind some of the most *fertile land* in all of Kemet.

"This river is our life Imhotep," his father would tell him.

"The Nile is more than just water for our crops, it fills our soup pots, gives us fish to eat, and guides our boats. Without it we wouldn't have papyrus for the precious scrolls you love to study so much."

Some of the first paper ever made, called *papyrus,* was from cyperus plants that grew along the great Nile river.

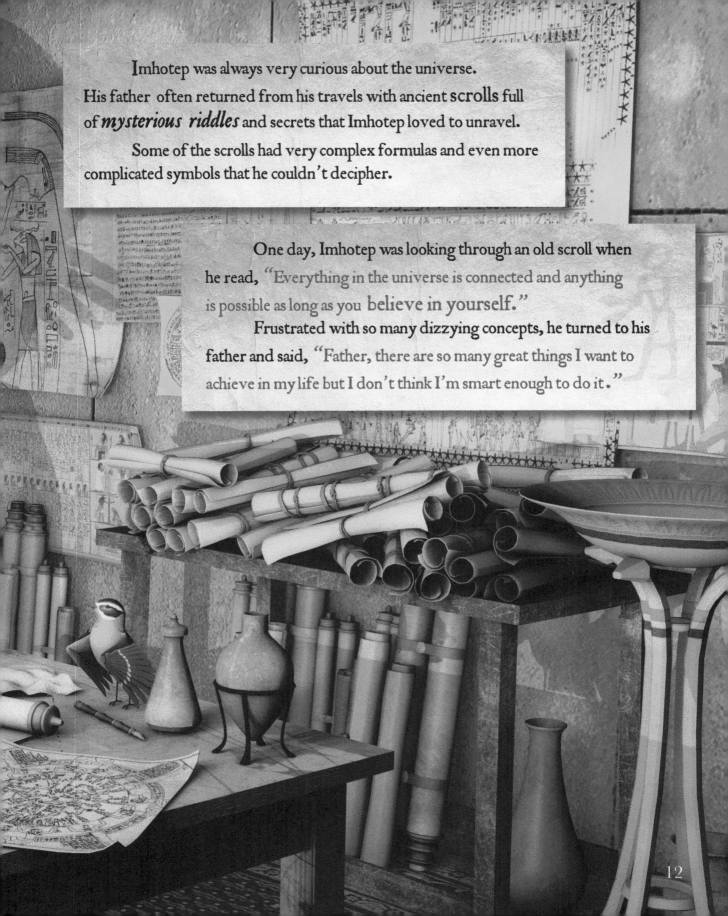

Imhotep was always very curious about the universe. His father often returned from his travels with ancient **scrolls** full of *mysterious riddles* and secrets that Imhotep loved to unravel.

Some of the scrolls had very complex formulas and even more complicated symbols that he couldn't decipher.

One day, Imhotep was looking through an old scroll when he read, "Everything in the universe is connected and anything is possible as long as you believe in yourself."

Frustrated with so many dizzying concepts, he turned to his father and said, "Father, there are so many great things I want to achieve in my life but I don't think I'm smart enough to do it."

Kanofer swiftly guided Imhotep outside to where the farmers were working and pointed to the buildings on the horizon.

"Son, when building a house, you always need a strong foundation and learning is the foundation for a strong mind.
If you want to make your dreams come true, the key is believing in yourself and letting the wonderful light inside of you shine."

"But, father I don't know if I believe," replied Imhotep.

"Be patient my son. You must plant the seeds, and tend to your garden, before you can harvest the fruits."

14

Everyday Imhotep went to school where he studied the complicated techniques of a *scribe*. A scribe was an expert that could read and write in complicated picture symbols called hieroglyphics.

For Imhotep, these symbols helped him better understand that imagination and *spirit was infinite* and had no limits.

Without limits in his mind, Imhotep noticed that his magical talents were growing more and more powerful. His spine tingled, his thoughts became focused, and a sparkling amber light began to illuminate from his palms.

It became clear to everyone who witnessed it, Imhotep had a special gift that needed to be shared with the people of Kemet.

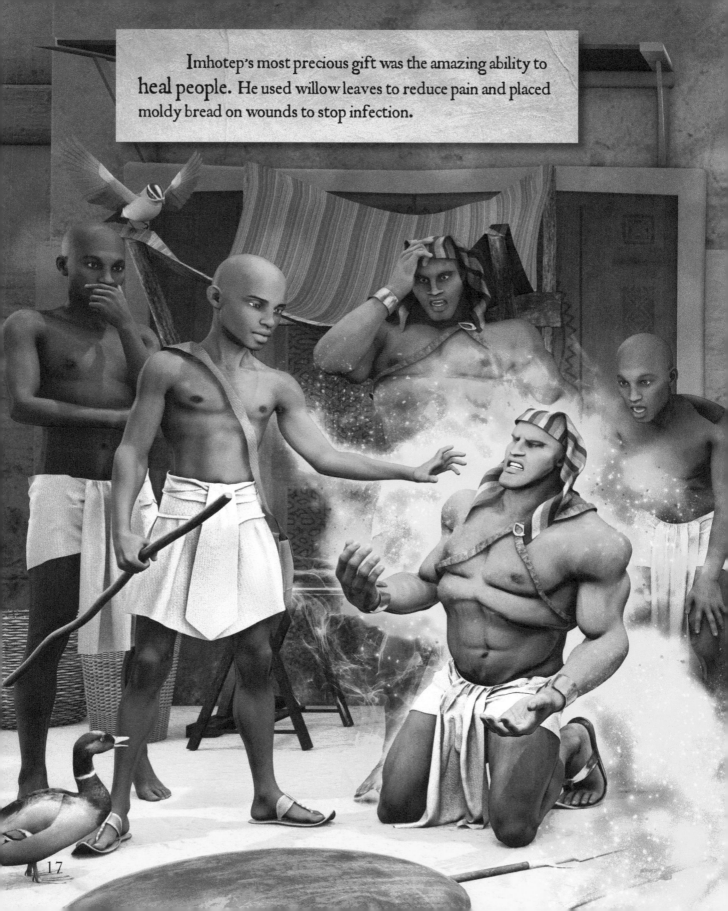

Imhotep's most precious gift was the amazing ability to heal people. He used willow leaves to reduce pain and placed moldy bread on wounds to stop infection.

17

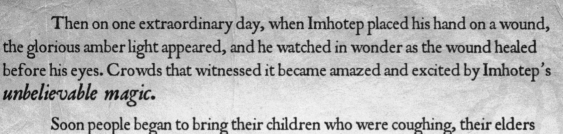

Then on one extraordinary day, when Imhotep placed his hand on a wound, the glorious amber light appeared, and he watched in wonder as the wound healed before his eyes. Crowds that witnessed it became amazed and excited by Imhotep's *unbelievable magic.*

Soon people began to bring their children who were coughing, their elders who were aching, and even warriors who were injured in battle.

The more Imhotep's inner light beamed with compassion, the more he could help the people of Kemet.

18

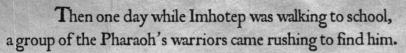

Then one day while Imhotep was walking to school, a group of the Pharaoh's warriors came rushing to find him.

"Imhotep! The Princess was stung by a venomous scorpion and now she has become very ill," yelled the warrior.

"None of the other doctors in Memphis can cure her. I told Pharaoh Zoser about your skills in magic, and he wants to see you immediately!"

At first, Imhotep was afraid to meet Pharaoh Zoser because he'd heard frightening stories about the King's short temper. But then he thought about the sick Princess and desperately wanted to help her.

Imhotep quickly grabbed his medicine bag, and the soldiers rushed him to the royal palace to see the Pharaoh.

When Imhotep entered the royal palace and saw the **Pharaoh**, the mighty ruler looked annoyed and angry.

"Who is this peasant I see before my eyes? Every noble doctor in Kemet is unable to cure my daughter. They have given up! My warriors say you are different. What makes you different than everyone else?" shouted Pharaoh Zoser.

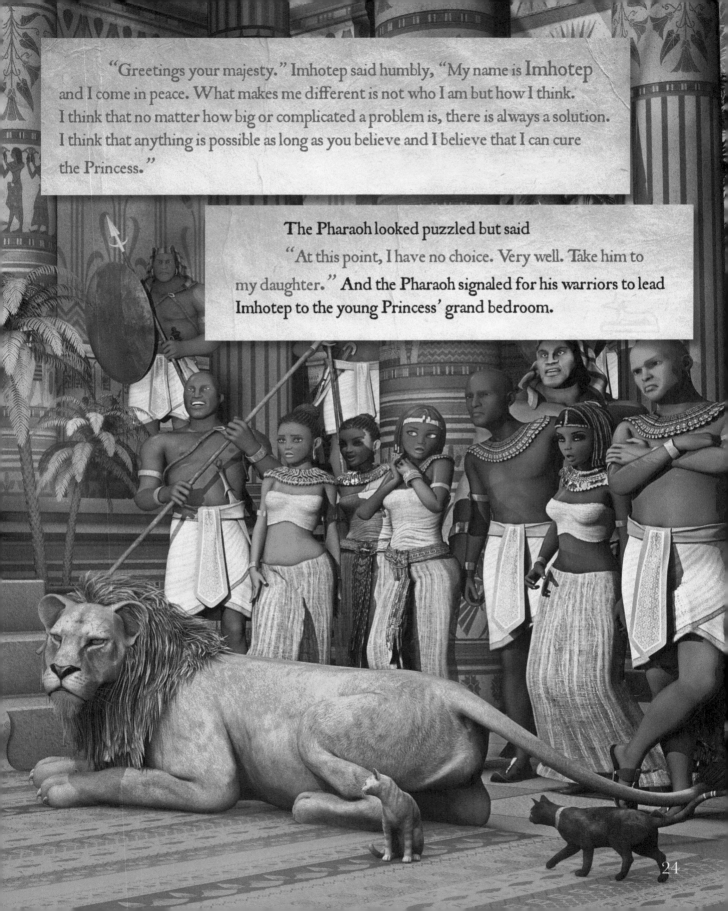

"Greetings your majesty." Imhotep said humbly, "My name is Imhotep and I come in peace. What makes me different is not who I am but how I think. I think that no matter how big or complicated a problem is, there is always a solution. I think that anything is possible as long as you believe and I believe that I can cure the Princess."

The Pharaoh looked puzzled but said "At this point, I have no choice. Very well. Take him to my daughter." And the Pharaoh signaled for his warriors to lead Imhotep to the young Princess' grand bedroom.

When Imhotep entered the room, he saw the young Princess weak with fever from the *scorpion's sting.*

He then asked the Queen, "Do you have the scorpion that bit her?" The queen replied, "Yes," and pointed to a dead scorpion in the corner.

25

Quickly, Imhotep picked up the scorpion and began crushing it with honey & herbs until it was liquid.

He then offered it to the princess to drink and placed his hand over her forehead.

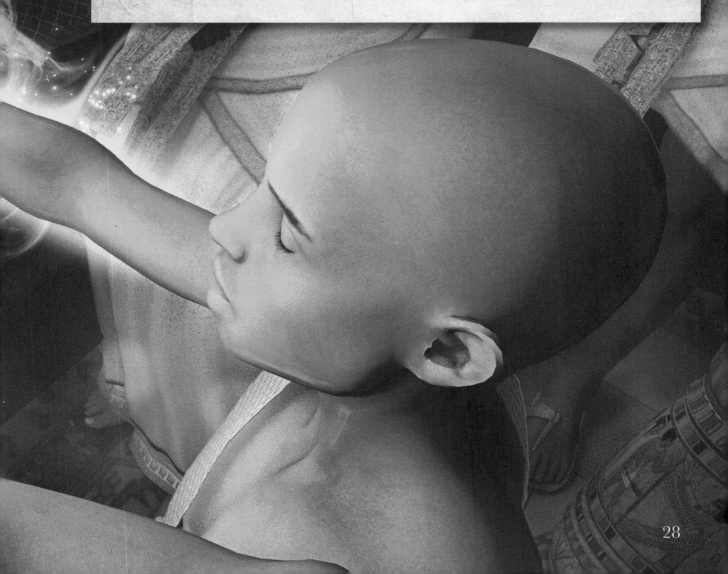

Imhotep closed his eyes and the room became silent. The palms of his hands began to glow brighter and brighter until the room was filled with a glorious light. As the light faded, the Princess' eyes fluttered open.

The Pharaoh, the Queen, and the guards were astonished as they watched her sit up and smile. *She had been cured!*

"Imhotep, you are a genius!" the Pharaoh proclaimed.

"Once I thought that having riches made a person wise. You have proven that knowledge can be found in anyone that is willing to learn and believe. From now on, you will be my personal advisor and live in the palace as my aid and the healer of Kemet!"

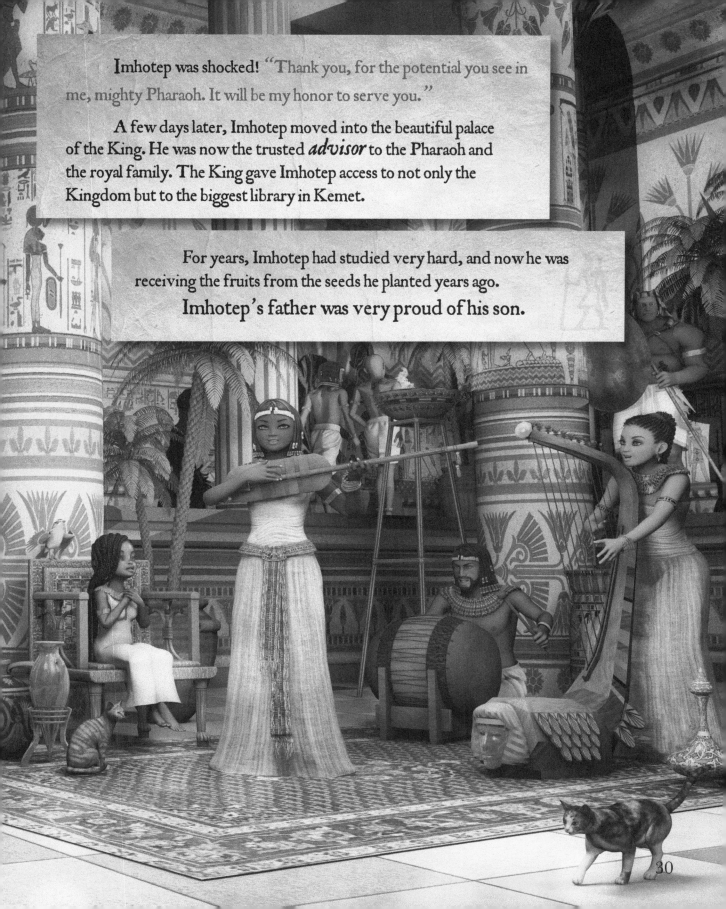

Imhotep was shocked! "Thank you, for the potential you see in me, mighty Pharaoh. It will be my honor to serve you."

A few days later, Imhotep moved into the beautiful palace of the King. He was now the trusted *advisor* to the Pharaoh and the royal family. The King gave Imhotep access to not only the Kingdom but to the biggest library in Kemet.

For years, Imhotep had studied very hard, and now he was receiving the fruits from the seeds he planted years ago.

Imhotep's father was very proud of his son.

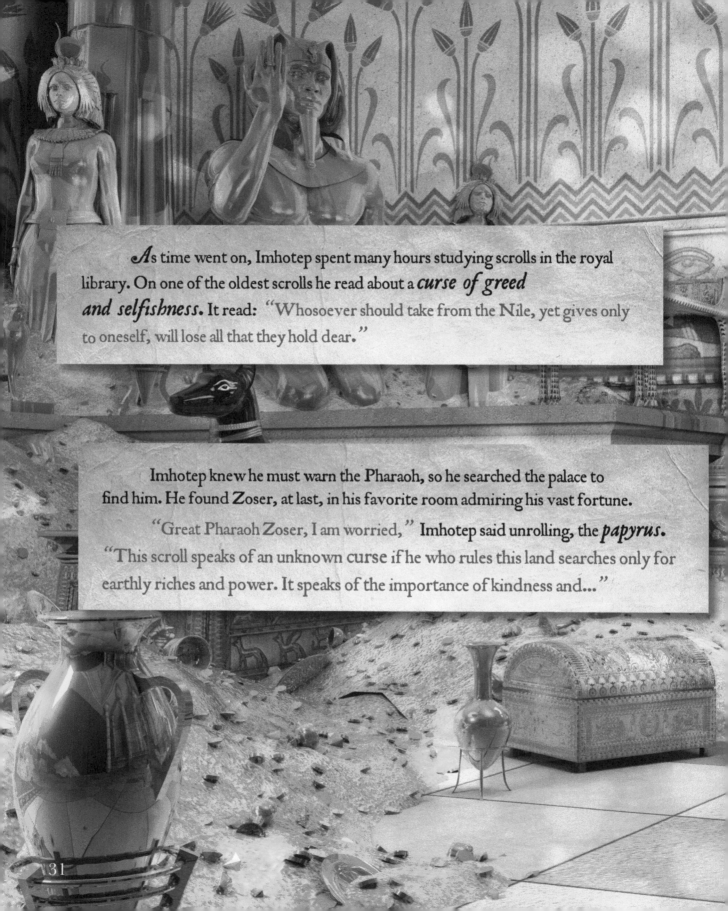

As time went on, Imhotep spent many hours studying scrolls in the royal library. On one of the oldest scrolls he read about a *curse of greed and selfishness.* It read: "Whosoever should take from the Nile, yet gives only to oneself, will lose all that they hold dear."

Imhotep knew he must warn the Pharaoh, so he searched the palace to find him. He found Zoser, at last, in his favorite room admiring his vast fortune.

"Great Pharaoh Zoser, I am worried," Imhotep said unrolling, the *papyrus.* "This scroll speaks of an unknown curse if he who rules this land searches only for earthly riches and power. It speaks of the importance of kindness and..."

"Silence!" the Pharaoh bellowed.

"The people of this land must be ruled with strength and power.
What good is kindness to a ruler? You cannot rule a nation with kindness."

32

*I*n seven short years, the sun of Kemet's glory days began to set as troubled times befell the kingdom and Pharaoh Zoser's empire turned to *gloom and sadness.*

The once beautiful and abundant Nile river had evaporated and now was drying up into a barren wasteland. The fertile soil was gone, crops began to die, and the people suffered from thirst and starvation.

Sorrow filled the King's heart because the children were no longer playing, brother robbed brother, and the kingdom was shriveling into dust.

The people of Kemet spoke only of the evil spirits that had cursed their land.

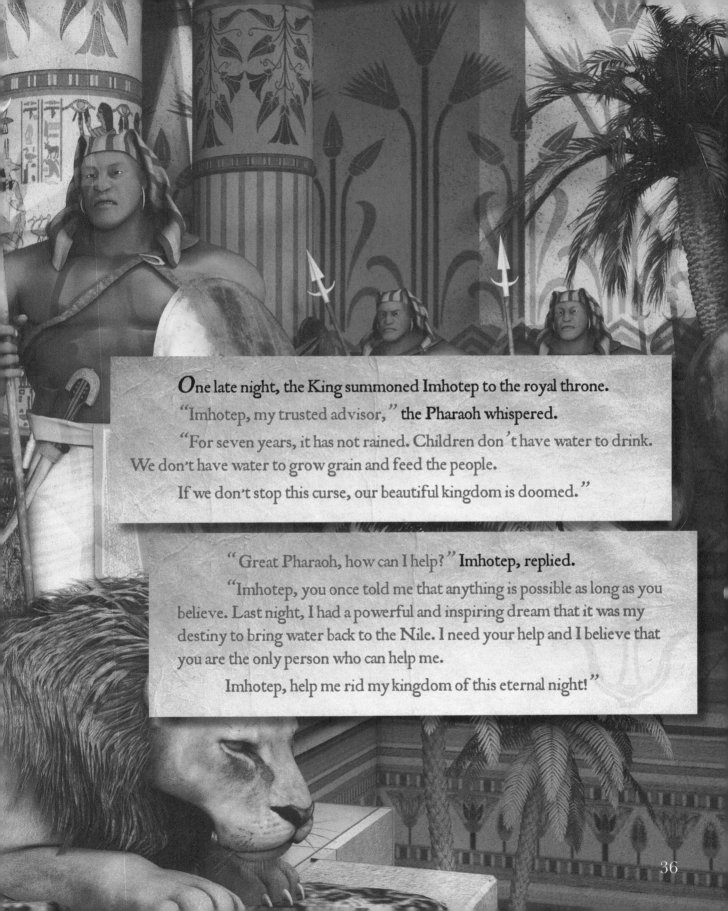

*O*ne late night, the King summoned Imhotep to the royal throne.

"Imhotep, my trusted advisor," the Pharaoh whispered.

"For seven years, it has not rained. Children don't have water to drink. We don't have water to grow grain and feed the people.

If we don't stop this curse, our beautiful kingdom is doomed."

"Great Pharaoh, how can I help?" Imhotep, replied.

"Imhotep, you once told me that anything is possible as long as you believe. Last night, I had a powerful and inspiring dream that it was my destiny to bring water back to the Nile. I need your help and I believe that you are the only person who can help me.

Imhotep, help me rid my kingdom of this eternal night!"

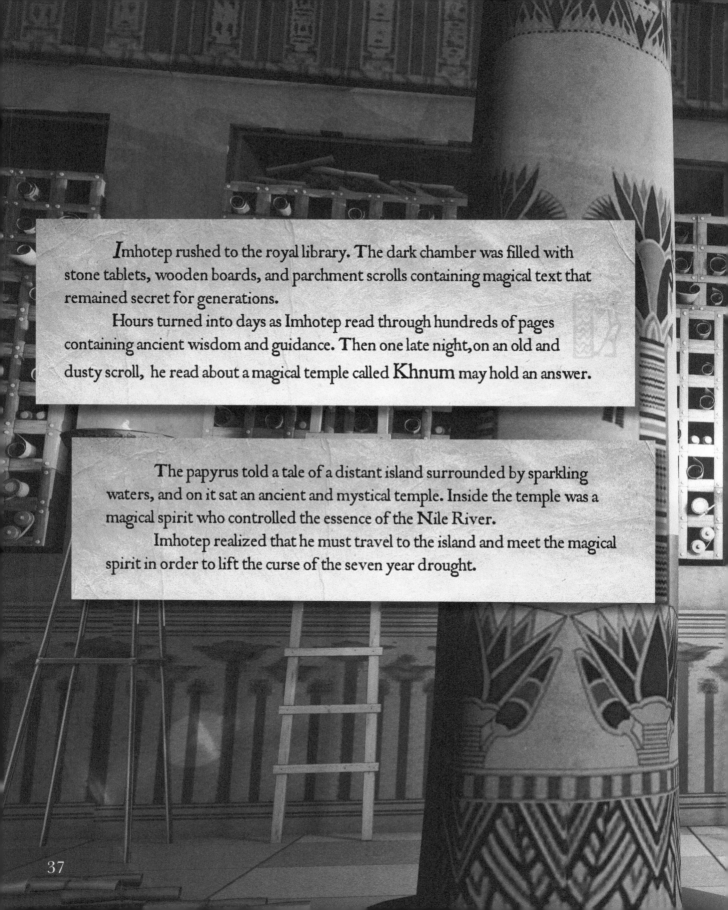

Imhotep rushed to the royal library. The dark chamber was filled with stone tablets, wooden boards, and parchment scrolls containing magical text that remained secret for generations.

Hours turned into days as Imhotep read through hundreds of pages containing ancient wisdom and guidance. Then one late night, on an old and dusty scroll, he read about a magical temple called Khnum may hold an answer.

The papyrus told a tale of a distant island surrounded by sparkling waters, and on it sat an ancient and mystical temple. Inside the temple was a magical spirit who controlled the essence of the Nile River.

Imhotep realized that he must travel to the island and meet the magical spirit in order to lift the curse of the seven year drought.

Imhotep took note of the temple's location and rushed back to the Pharaoh to explain his plan.

"Imhotep, this is a dangerous journey," said the Pharaoh as he listened to Imhotep's plan.

"Are you sure you can find the temple?"

"Yes, mighty Zoser!" he said "I will travel south along the Nile River toward Nubia. Once the river is high enough I'll use the stars as my compass to find the temple. I will not fail the people of Kemet."

And so it was planned, and when the orange light of the desert morning rose from the East, Imhotep set out on his long journey toward the island of Khnum.

He traveled south toward Nubia and rode a camel that was specially requested by the Pharaoh. In Kemet, most people used donkeys and horses but Imhotep read that camels could travel faster than horses and go days without drinking water.

After battling through hot winds and brutal sandstorms, Imhotep eventually reached the shore closest to the island.

The southern Nile shore had become a dark, deep swamp and Imhotep needed a way to get across it. The water was especially dangerous because it was filled with venomous snakes and spiders, vicious hippos and deadly crocodiles.

While standing at the shore, Imhotep saw an old papyrus boat stuck in the tall reeds. He swiftly seized the boat and began paddling toward the island.

44

As the night approached, heavy winds began to toss the boat back and forth across the waves.

Hungry crocodiles surrounded him and snapped their ferocious jaws like savage demons. Imhotep was startled and almost thrown into the water but he remained calm. He focused all of his energy on blinding them with the brilliant light from his hands. Shocked and confused by the blazing light from Imhotep, the crocodiles swam away in fear.

The river raged but with Imhotep's skillful navigation he made it safely to the shore of the island. Carefully, Imhotep climbed over the rocks at the water's edge and began hiking up the side of the mountain. Once he arrived at the top, he saw the the ancient temple of Khnum.

Before him was the temple that no one had entered in hundreds of years.

Imhotep took a deep breath and summoned every ounce of courage he had left as he carefully walked past the fierce looking stone guardians of the temple, figures he'd only ever seen from the safety of the Pharaoh's library.

48

As Imhotep made his way through the dark twisting hallways, he could barely see where he was going. Knowing that the hieroglyphics on the temple walls could help to guide him, Imhotep used his golden light to ignite the candles throughout the temple.

The inscriptions guided Imhotep through the corridors and helped him avoid booby traps meant to catch robbers and bandits. At every turn, he came across the bones and skulls of the greedy and selfish who hadn't read the warnings on the walls.

He finally made his way to the altar of Khnum when a sudden gust of wind blew through the temple and extinguished the candles. In the blink of an eye it became so dark, that Imhotep couldn't even see his own hands.

51

Just before panic set in, a **magnificent spirit** appeared to Imhotep.

"Who has disturbed the temple of Khnum?" yelled the great spirit.

Towering above Imhotep rose the intimidating figure that he'd seen only in ancient and secret scrolls.

With the head of a **ram** and the body of a man, mighty Khnum held a scepter as if he could strike at any moment. "Mighty Khnum, my name is Imhotep and *I come in peace.* I was sent by the great Pharaoh Zoser. We need your help to bring water back to the Nile."

Khnum's laugh filled the temple and shook the walls.

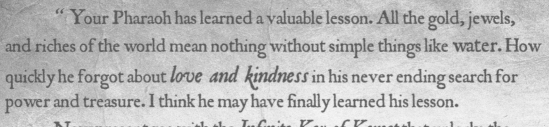

" Your Pharaoh has learned a valuable lesson. All the gold, jewels, and riches of the world mean nothing without simple things like water. How quickly he forgot about *love and kindness* in his never ending search for power and treasure. I think he may have finally learned his lesson.

Now present me with the *Infinite Key of Kemet* that unlocks the Universe and the Nile will flow with water once again." Imhotep gasped!

The **Infinite Key of Kemet** that unlocks the universe? What is that? He thought. He had come hundreds of miles but didn't know he needed a key!

Had he come this far only to fail?

Imhotep fell to his knees, closed his eyes, and thought about all of the suffering people in Kemet that he let down. He thought about the Pharaoh, his father, and all of the experiences that brought him to this point.

Then he remembered something his **father told him** when we was young, a valuable lesson that was so much a part of his life.

Imhotep spoke in a calm strong voice.

"The infinite key that unlocks the universe is *my mind.*" he said

"My mind has no limits. I can achieve anything in life as long as I use my mind and *believe in myself.*"

Suddenly, in a wisp of smoke appeared a glorious light that rose higher and higher in the still darkened temple before exploding and raining down upon him, as beautiful as the rain that had already started to fall from the sky.

The curse had been broken!

Imhotep returned to Kemet and the Pharaoh was overjoyed. The palace came to life with rejoicing and cheering crowds gathered in ront of the doors and throughout the streets. King Zoser smiled, embraced Imhotep, and escorted him inside the palace.

Then he lead Imhotep to the royal courtyard overlooking the entire kingdom and began to speak.

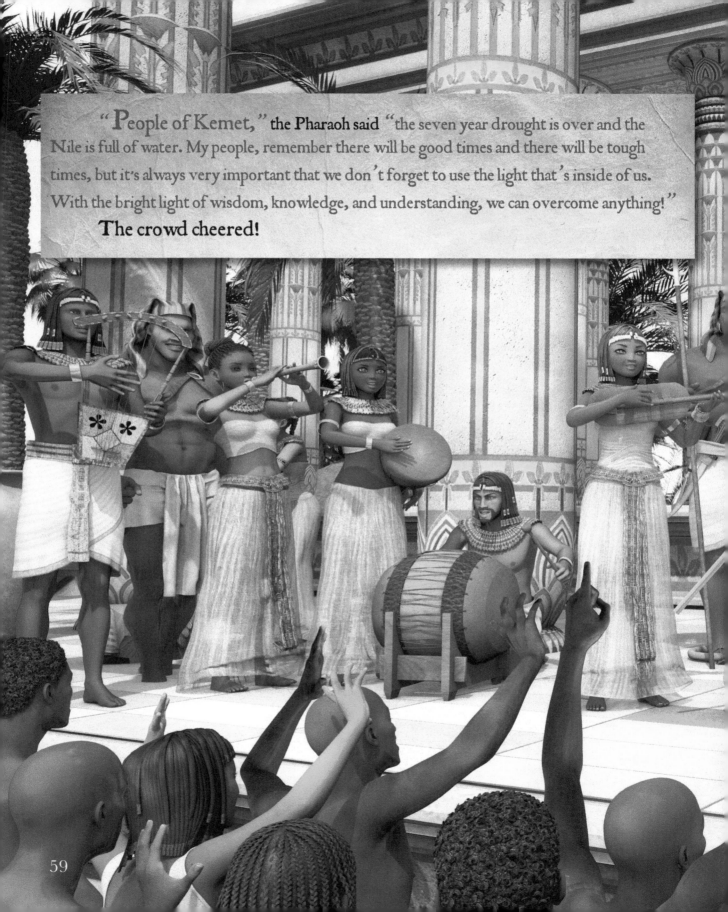

"People of Kemet," the Pharaoh said "the seven year drought is over and the Nile is full of water. My people, remember there will be good times and there will be tough times, but it's always very important that we don't forget to use the light that's inside of us. With the bright light of wisdom, knowledge, and understanding, we can overcome anything!"

The crowd cheered!

The Pharaoh continued, "this was not something I have always known but something I was taught by my most trusted advisor and good friend, Imhotep! All hail Imhotep!"
The crowd cheered again,

"Imhotep! Imhotep!"

GLOSSARY

Hieroglyphics
The formal writing system used in Ancient Egypt.

Imhotep
An ancient Egyptian genius who achieved great success in a wide variety of fields. Inventor of the pyramid, author of ancient wisdom, architect, high priest, physician, astronomer, and magician, Imhotep's many talents and vast acquired knowledge had such an effect on the Egyptian people that he later became celebrated as a god.

Kanofer
Imhotep's father, a great architect, who was later known to be the first of a long line of master builders who contributed to building Egyptian temples.

Kemet
The Ancient Egyptian word for Egypt which translates to the "black land" or "the land of the blacks".

Khnum
An ancient Egyptian god who was originally the god of the source of the Nile. Khnum was usually depicted with the head of a ram and a body of a man.

Nile River
One of the longest rivers in the world and also called the father of African rivers.

Nubia
A region along the Nile river encompassing the area between southern Egypt and central Sudan. Nubia was one of the earliest civilizations of ancient Africa, with a history that can be traced back to 2500 BC.

Papyrus
Egyptians used fibers of the cyperus plant to make a flat material they could write and paint on. The word "paper" comes from "papyrus".

Pharaoh
The name of a ruler or king in ancient Egypt. A Pharaoh owned all of the land, enacted laws, collected taxes, and defended the kingdom from invaders.

Scribe
A trained expert that could read and write in complicated picture symbols called hieroglyphics.

Statue of Seated Imhotep
(332 BC)

Writings in Imhotep's Tomb
(332-200 BC)

Egyptian Wall Paintings
(1350 BC)

ALSO AVAILABLE:

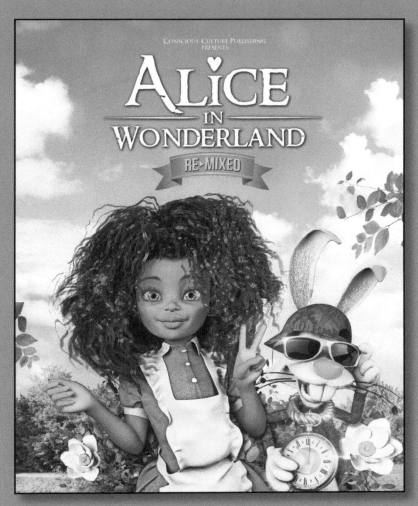

Alice in Wonderland Remixed is a modern retelling of the Lewis Carroll classic with diverse subject matter and the conscious flavor of black girl magic.

Download the E-Book for FREE:

www.consciousculturepublishing.com
www.facebook.com/ConsciousCultr
@ConsciousCultr

CPSIA information can be obtained
at www.ICGtesting.com
Printed in the USA
LVHW071953150723
752125LV00019B/144